The Surprise Disguise

Thelma Lambert

Illustrated by

Margaret Chamberlain

Hamish Hamilton
London

In memory of Thelma

M.C.

HAMISH HAMILTON LTD

Published by the Penguin Group
27 Wrights Lane, London w8 5TZ, England
Penguin Books USA Inc., 375 Hudson Street, New York, New York 10014, USA
Penguin Books Australia Ltd, Ringwood, Victoria, Australia
Penguin Books Canada Ltd, 10 Alcorn Avenue, Toronto, Ontario, Canada M4V 3B2
Penguin Books (NZ) Ltd, 182–190 Wairau Road, Auckland 10, New Zealand

Penguin Books Ltd, Registered Offices: Harmondsworth, Middlesex, England

First published in Great Britain 1997 by Hamish Hamilton Ltd

1 3 5 7 9 10 8 6 4 2

British Library Cataloguing in Publication Data
CIP data for this book is available from the British Library

ISBN 0-241-00296-6

Set in 15pt Plantin by
Rowland Phototypesetting Ltd, Bury St Edmunds, Suffolk

Printed in China by Imago Publishing

Rupert Davis sat miserably at his desk,
trying to work.

"It's no good, Miss," he groaned. "I just
can't do joined-up writing . . ."

Miss Smith came over to look at his work
and sighed. Rupert's writing looked as if a
spider had dipped itself in ink and crawled
slowly and painfully across the page. Poor
Rupert! He was by far the worst in the class
at things like reading and writing.

To make matters worse, Rupert was very big for his age – almost as big as Miss Smith, his teacher. So of course everyone expected him to be able to do things like someone who was much older. Things like your thirteen-times-table, and knowing all the dates of the Kings and Queens of England. Things like joined-up writing.

No, what Rupert Davis really liked doing
was dressing-up. And acting. Rupert's
granny had been an actress, and at home
he had an enormous dressing-up box. His
granny had filled it with hats and boots,
velvet dresses, pirate hooks and silver
swords, all jumbled up together.

Rupert had hours of fun dressing up, and
pretending to be different people.
Sometimes he would act out a little play for
his mum and dad. But at school, Rupert
didn't get much chance to dress up –
specially now he was in the Juniors. Just
once a year at Christmas, when they all
trooped into the village church and put on a
Nativity play. *That* was fun . . . Groaning
to himself, Rupert bent over his work book

again, and once more the inky spider walked painfully across the page.

The following Monday when Miss Smith came into the classroom she had some exciting news for Class Two.

"Angela Buxted, the author of the famous *Danny the Dolphin* books, is staying with the vicar. And you will all be delighted to hear that Miss Buxted has promised to visit our class on Friday afternoon."

Miss Smith said the famous author would tell the children how she got her ideas for her stories.

"I've got *Danny the Dolphin Goes to the Moon*," said a small girl in the front row. "Will Angela Buxted sign it for me?"

Lots of other people had copies of *Danny the Dolphin* books. Would the famous author sign these, too?

"Of course!" beamed Miss Smith. "Now, we have the rest of the week to prepare for Miss Buxted's visit. I suggest we have a nice display of her books in the Library Corner.

Any other ideas, Class Two?"

"We could write reviews of her books,"
said an earnest boy who loved writing.

"We could make fairy cakes for her tea,"
said a girl who loved cooking. "With pink
icing."

"We could paint pictures of what we
think she'll look like," said the best artist in
the class.

"Yes, YES!' cried Miss Smith, clapping
her hands. "What *super* ideas!"

The teacher seemed as excited as anyone by the thought of the famous author's visit.

There followed four days of feverish activity in Miss Smith's class. Cakes were baked for the great author's tea, portraits of Miss Buxted were painted, and her books were tastefully arranged in the Library Corner. Everyone wrote a review of their favourite *Danny the Dolphin* book.

By Friday lunchtime, everything was in perfect readiness for The Visit. Miss Smith gazed round the classroom in satisfaction. The portraits on the walls were bold and well painted, the tea table, with its lace cloth, pink iced cakes and milk in a jug, looked very tempting. The book reviews were well written with hardly any spelling mistakes.

"You've all done very well," called the teacher, as the children put on their coats to go home for lunch. "I'm so proud of you! Angela Buxted will be most impressed, I'm sure."

Everyone hurried homewards, chattering excitedly about the Big Event of the afternoon. In Class Two's room, only Rupert Davis still lingered, putting the finishing touches to his picture of the famous author. Very carefully, he added large hoop ear-rings to his portrait. Enormous ear-rings, the size of digestive biscuits.

It was just as Rupert was going out through the school gate that it happened. The vicar came hurrying up the road, mopping his brow.

"Ah, Rupert, isn't it?" he panted. "Look my boy, I have an urgent message for your teacher – Miss What's-her-name – "

"Miss Smith," said Rupert.

"Yes. Could you tell Miss Smith that I'm terribly sorry but Angela Buxted won't be able to visit today after all? She's been called away to London rather suddenly. I do hope you haven't all gone to a lot of trouble. Must dash – " Still mopping his brow, the Reverend Wilkins rushed off to catch the one o'clock bus which had just roared into the village.

Rupert walked slowly home. Hoped they
hadn't gone to a lot of trouble! *Well*. He
liked *that*! Hadn't they thought of nothing
else for days? Hadn't they made cakes,
painted pictures, written reviews? Not gone
to any trouble, indeed!

Rupert thought how disappointed all the
children would be. Even Miss Smith –
especially Miss Smith! She'd be the most
disappointed of all. Now Rupert was a kind
boy. And he liked his teacher. It upset him

to think of her going to all that trouble for
nothing.

Rupert stopped dead in the middle of the
pavement. Then he punched the air three
times in triumph. He'd just had an idea – a
really FANTASTIC idea! He ran all the
rest of the way home, up the stairs two at a
time, and flung open his dressing-up
box . . .

"May I introduce the famous author, Miss
Angela Buxted?"

Mr Collins, the head teacher of St Mary's
School, came into Class Two's form room,
followed by a small, round lady in an
enormous flowered hat.

Every eye was fastened on the strange
little figure which had followed the Head
into the room. It tottered on very high heels,
adjusting its belt, its bosoms, its hat, its
over large, horn-rimmed spectacles as it
went, finally sinking
gratefully into the
teacher's comfy chair.
A flower from the
enormous hat dangled
over one eye, a fox
fur hung down from
her shoulders, and
enormous silver
ear-rings jangled
from her
ears.

"Can I say what a great honour it is to have you visit us," beamed Miss Smith. "We're all great fans of yours in Class Two, aren't we?"

"YES!" roared the children.

The famous author smiled and nodded and waved, rather like the Queen from the balcony of Buckingham Palace.

"I wonder if we might start with a few questions," said Miss Smith brightly. "Can you tell us how you get your ideas for your wonderful *Danny the Dolphin* books?"

The author began to speak in a strange, gruff voice.

"I keep a dolphin in the bath at home," she said. "He's called Danny."

"It must be a very – large bath," faltered Miss Smith.

"It is," said the great author coldly.

"Very large. And when I wrote *Danny Goes to the Moon*, I went there with him so's I could see what the moon was like."

"And what was it like?" said Miss Smith faintly.

"It was like snow on the moon. Only it doesn't melt," said the author. "Danny gives me all my ideas. I can speak Dolphin."

"Can you speak some now?" said a young hopeful at the back.

Miss Buxted thought for a moment.

"Oogla, doogla, waller galloo," she said gruffly. "Ucka, gucka, gob."

The girl who loved cooking put up her hand.

"What does Danny the Dolphin eat?" she said.

"Lamb chops," said the famous author firmly.

Soon it was time for the children to have their copies of the *Danny* books signed.

"Queue up quietly!" cried Miss Smith.

The first child was Donna Wilson. And she wanted a message written in her book.

"Can you put 'To Donna with love from Angela Buxted', please?"

Everyone crowded round to watch as the famous author began to write. A murmur ran round the class: Miss Buxted was printing the message in capitals!

"I don't do joined-up," she said sternly.

Then, "How do you spell 'Buxted'? Does it have a 'k' in it?"

Everyone roared with laughter.

"You have a great sense of humour," said Miss Smith. "Now children, give Miss Buxted some room. Go and sit down when you've had your book signed."

The author didn't seem interested in reading the reviews of her books.

"I don't want to wear my eyes out with too much reading," she said, pushing the outsized spectacles back up her nose. "They're already worn out with all that writing of my books, see."

But the author did graciously admire the portraits of herself on the walls. She particularly liked the one with the very big ear-rings, signed 'Rupert'.

"Now we've prepared you a little afternoon tea," said Miss Smith. "The children have made cakes specially."

The class watched in awe as quantities of pink iced cakes began to disappear at great speed under the brim of the enormous hat.

But Miss Buxted waved away the proffered cup of tea.

"Don't drink that stuff," she said gruffly. "Got any cola?"

After a while Miss Angela Buxted looked pointedly at her enormous watch, and muttered that she had to be going.

"But before I go – " She signalled to Miss Smith and whispered something in her ear. It appeared that the famous author had a sudden, urgent need to go to the toilet.

"It's all right, I know where it is," said Miss Buxted hoarsely, struggling to her feet. But she was suddenly flummoxed: was she meant to go to the girls' toilet?

"Let me show you to the staff toilet," murmured the teacher, with a twinkle in her eye. "This way, Miss Buxted . . ."

The famous author began to totter towards the door. But those very high heels – that very long dress – WHAM! Getting hopelessly tangled up, the author fell heavily to the ground, letting out a piercing scream.

The enormous hat fell off. The fox fur fell off. The huge glasses fell off. And there, spread-eagled on the floor, was revealed – Rupert Davis. He sat up and said a Very Rude Word.

"RUPERT!" gasped Miss Smith.

"How people walk in those shoes I'll never know," he moaned. "I think I've broken my ankle!"

Miss Smith was not as cross as she might have been. She said she understood that Rupert had done it with the very best of intentions; so she only gave him a short ticking-off. But it had been worth it – those cakes had been absolutely delicious. And everyone had had a good laugh. Rupert loved making people laugh.

The children of Class Two streamed out
of school at the end of the day as they
always did – whooping and running and
pushing each other. But this Friday
afternoon there was a new element added.
As they went their noisy way, strange
words could be heard echoing all round the
village:

"OOGLA, DOOGLA, WALLER
GALLOO . . . UCKA, GUCKA, GOB!"

Good old Rupert.